PAPI'S GIFT

Karen Stanton
Illustrated by
René King Moreno

BOYDS MILLS PRESS
AN IMPRINT OF HIGHLIGHTS
Honesdale, Pennsylvania

Boyds Mills Press
An Imprint of Highlights
815 Church Street
Honesdale, Pennsylvania 18431
Printed in China

Library of Congress Cataloging-in-Publication Data

Stanton, Karen.
    Papi's gift / by Karen Stanton ; illustrated by René King Moreno.—1st ed.
        p. cm.
    Summary: Graciela's Papi has been working in the United States for so long that she has almost forgotten
his face, so when the box he promised for her seventh birthday does not arrive, she is very upset and nearly
loses hope that he—and the rain—will someday return.
    ISBN-13: 978-1-59078-422-8 (hardcover : alk. paper)
    [1. Fathers and daughters—Fiction. 2. Birthdays—Fiction.
3. Droughts—Fiction. 4. Mexico—Fiction.] I. Moreno, René King, ill. II. Title.
PZ7.S79328Pap 2007
[E]—dc22
                                    2006011569

First edition
The text of this book is set in 14-point Sabon.
The illustrations are done in pastel.
10 9 8 7 6 5 4 3

For Will, Raul, Gabriela, and all our friends
in San Andrés Itzapa, Guatemala

—KS

For Tomás, Olivia's *papi*

—RKM

It is hot and dry on the day that Papi tells me about the box.
"Graciela," he says, "I have sent you a box—a big box full of wonderful things for my girl on her seventh birthday."

I jump up and down, clap my hands, and drop the telephone that hangs on the wall outside Tio Julio's market. My papi has sent a box from the United States just for me. He says he tied it up with red string because red is my favorite color. He wrote my name on it in big letters: Graciela María Reyes Rivera.

Papi says I have to be patient. He has only enough money to send my box on a slow mail truck. Papi won't tell me what is inside the box. He says it should be a surprise.

Every day I wait for my box to arrive. While I milk our goat, Blanca, my eyes watch for the dust cloud that follows the mail truck. Mama boils the milk for our breakfast while her eyes search the sky for rain.

Our crops couldn't grow without rain. The corn and the
peanuts all turned brown and died. No food to sell at market.
No food for our chickens or our cows. No food for my papi,
my mama, my brothers, or me.

So Papi left to pick the fruit in faraway California. Now
he sends us money to buy the things we need.

I don't remember when I stopped counting the days without
Papi. He has been gone so long that I am forgetting his face.
I ask Mama to show me their wedding photograph. Papi is big
and smiling. Mama is small and serious.

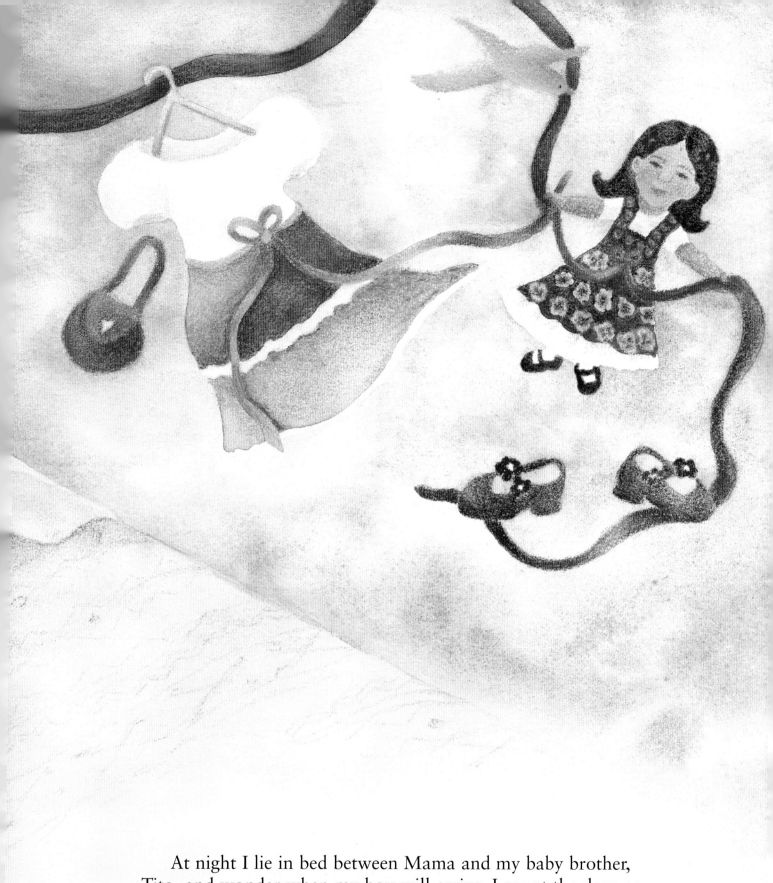

At night I lie in bed between Mama and my baby brother, Tito, and wonder when my box will arrive. I count the days on my fingers and then on my toes and then on the fingers and toes of little Tito. I dream about a giant box filled with fancy party dresses, shiny new shoes, and a doll with real hair to braid. But my box does not arrive.

One hot morning, Mama takes us to the market to wait for Papi's call. It's not Sunday like usual. It is Friday—my birthday. When I hear Papi's voice, I know something is wrong.

"My daughter," Papi says, "I'm sorry your box has not arrived for your birthday. Graciela, I'm afraid it must be lost."

"No, Papi," I say. "Don't say that. You promised me it would be here for my birthday." The phone falls from my ear, and I glare at Mama. She hands the telephone back to me, and I hear something I have never heard before: the sound of my papi crying.

Then with his strange, sad voice, Papi sings to me. "Happy birthday. *Feliz cumpleaños*, Graciela."

But I don't care that it's my birthday. I don't care if my papi is sad. I don't care if the rain never comes again to our house. I don't talk to Mama all day. I sit on the sweaty back of our burro, Chilo. I won't come inside.

When Chilo gets thirsty, I take him down to the almost-dried-up river where Papi taught me and Pedro how to swim. Chilo dips his nose in the muddy pool that used to be our swimming hole. I twirl and spin on the swing that Papi made for us out of rope and an old tire. I almost forget about my box.

I pull Chilo home.

Mama and my brothers are waiting for me with a birthday dinner.

Mama made my favorite treat, *arroz con leche*. After dinner we sing, but we don't talk about my box. I think about my papi alone in California.

I hope he is not crying still.

Then Mama hands me a small package wrapped in newspaper.
She smiles. Mama's smile has been hiding since Papi had to go away.
"*Feliz cumpleaños, mi hija,*" Mama says. I tear the paper to see what
is inside. A doll. But not the beautiful doll from the box in my dreams.

I touch the doll with my finger. I don't look at Mama. It is a doll that she has made out of dried corn husks and scraps from my worn-out dresses.

Mama lifts the doll out of the newspaper and hands her to me. My fingers touch something soft on top of the doll's head— braids of silky brown hair, real hair that Mama saved from my last trim.

I look at Mama and smile. "*Gracias*, Mama," I say, giving her a hug. "*Muchas, muchas gracias.*"

I love my doll and I name her Perdita.
When the long, hot summer is almost over and Mama
has sewn the buttons back onto Perdita's dress twice,
I stop waiting for my box. I know now it is lost.

"Mama," I say, "when will Papi come home again?"

"One day, Graciela," Mama says. "When the rain comes back,
you will see your papi again."

What if the rain never comes again? Then our crops will stay brown and dry. My papi will stay alone in the United States. We will listen to his voice on the pay phone at Tio Julio's market on Sundays forever.

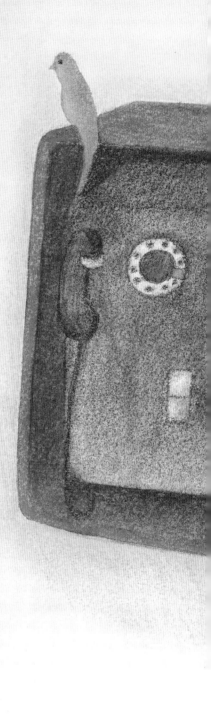

The next day, I go down to the market with Perdita and a pocket full of pesos that I have been saving for something important. Tío Julio says seven pesos is just about enough for a box with a red string and stamps for the United States. I kiss Perdita's silky hair and place her inside the box on a soft bed of torn newspapers. I wish I could climb inside the box with her. I will miss her.

"You will love the United States, Perdita," I say. "And you will love my papi." I tell her I will see her again when the rains come.

I wave *adiós* to Perdita and watch the mail truck carry Papi's gift away across the dry desert.

I wait until the dust cloud disappears. Then I head home to tell Mama about Perdita.

But in the middle of the dusty road I stop. Something feels different today, and I look out over the desert and dry arroyos toward the red mountains. The sky is the same as every day, clear blue and full of heat. Then a sudden breeze cools the back of my neck. I turn and dust blows into my eyes.

When I open them again, I run to tell Mama what I see.

Clouds.

Dark clouds rolling across the dry desert. Clouds that may soon bring rain.

And after that . . . I hope . . .

my papi.